3/14

GRINNELL LIBRARY ASSOC

S0-AHO-972

Superhero
Ed!

Level 6B

Grinnell Library
2642 East Main Street
Wappingers Falls, NY 12590
845-297-3428

Written by Louise Goodman
Illustrated by Kimberley Scott
Reading Consultant: Betty Franchi

About Phonics

Spoken English uses more than 40 speech sounds. Each sound is called a *phoneme*. Some phonemes relate to a single letter (d-o-g) and others to combinations of letters (sh-ar-p). When a phoneme is written down, it is called a *grapheme*. Teaching these sounds, matching them to their written form, and sounding out words for reading is the basis of phonics.

Early phonics instruction gives children the tools to sound out, blend, and say the words without having to rely on memory or guesswork. This instruction gives children the confidence and ability to read unfamiliar words, helping them progress toward independent reading.

About the Consultant

Betty Franchi is an American educator with a Bachelor's Degree in Elementary and Middle Education as well as a Master's Degree in Special Education. Betty holds a National Boards for Professional Teaching Standards certification. Throughout her 24 years as a teacher, she has studied and developed an expertise in Phonetic Awareness and has implemented phonetic strategies, teaching many young children to read, including students with special needs.

Reading tips

This book focuses on two sounds made with the letter *e* (as in b**e**d) and *ee* (as in h**e**).

Tricky and/or new words in this book

Any words in bold may have unusual spellings or are new and have not yet been introduced.

> **Tricky and/or new words in this book**
>
> **scheming**

Extra ways to have fun with this book

After the readers have finished the story, ask them questions about what they have just read.

What kind of animal is Meg?
Can you remember two words that contain the different sounds shown by the letter e?

I could be Superhero Ed's companion, Sidekick Fred!

A Pronunciation Guide

This grid contains the sounds used in the stories in levels 4, 5, and 6 and a guide on how to say them.

/ă/ as in pat	/ā/ as in pay	/âr/ as in care	/ä/ as in father
/b/ as in bib	/ch/ as in church	/d/ as in deed/ milled	/ĕ/ as in pet
/ē/ as in bee	/f/ as in fife/ phase/ rough	/g/ as in gag	/h/ as in hat
/hw/ as in which	/ĭ/ as in pit	/ī/ as in pie/ by	/îr/ as in pier
/j/ as in judge	/k/ as in kick/ cat/ pique	/l/ as in lid/ needle (nēd'l)	/m/ as in mom
/n/ as in no/ sudden (sŭd'n)	/ng/ as in thing	/ŏ/ as in pot	/ō/ as in toe
/ô/ as in caught/ paw/ for/ horrid/ hoarse	/oi/ as in noise	/o͝o/ as in took	/ū/ as in cute

/ou/ as in **ou**t	/p/ as in **p**o**p**	/r/ as in **r**oa**r**	/s/ as in **s**au**ce**
/sh/ as in **sh**ip/ di**sh**	/t/ as in **t**igh**t**/ stopp**ed**	/th/ as in **th**in	/th/ as in **th**is
/ŭ/ as in c**u**t	/ûr/ as in **ur**ge/ t**er**m/ f**ir**m/ w**or**d/ h**ear**d	/v/ as in **v**al**v**e	/w/ as in **w**ith
/y/ as in **y**es	/z/ as in **z**ebra/ **x**ylem	/zh/ as in vi**s**ion/ plea**s**ure/ gara**ge**/	/ə/ as in **a**bout/ it**e**m/ edibl**e**/ gall**o**p/ circ**u**s
/ər/ as in butt**er**			

Be careful not to add an /uh/ sound to /s/, /t/, /p/, /c/, /h/, /r/, /m/, /d/, /g/, /l/, /f/ and /b/. For example, say /ff/ not /fuh/ and /sss/ not /suh/.

Ed was the best superhero you would ever meet. He had a special red vest and a cape with sequins.

He could fight villains and save the world. The worst villain was Wicked Ted. He was a **scheming** villain.

One day Superhero Ed heard
a scream. He jumped over the bed.
He jumped over the desk.
He even jumped over the fence.

"What's wrong, Deb?"

"Wicked Ted has taken Emu Meg.
I don't know where they could be.
Help me, I beg you!" she said.

Superhero Ed followed the trail.
It led to a dead end. Superhero Ed
saw Wicked Ted with Emu Meg.

They were in a plane.
Superhero Ed jumped over the wall.
He jumped over the lamppost.
He even jumped over the tree.

The plane landed in the sea.
Wicked Ted jumped onto a boat.

Grinnell Library
2642 East Main Street
Wappingers Falls, NY 12590
845-297-3428

Superhero Ed grabbed Emu Meg,
but just then the boat rocked.

They all fell in. "Help! I can't swim,"
cried Wicked Ted.

"Neither can I!" said Superhero Ed.
Deb arrived in time. "I can," she said.

Deb helped them onto the boat.

"Emu Meg!" she said,
giving her a hug.

"Wicked Ted, you must behave,"
she said. "I'm sorry. I will,"
said Wicked Ted.

"Thank you Superhero Ed," she said.
Superhero Ed just smiled.

Superhero Ed jumped over the fence.
He jumped over the desk. He jumped
into bed. What a busy day for
Superhero Ed.

OVER 48 TITLES IN SIX LEVELS
Betty Franchi recommends...

Other titles to enjoy from Level 4

978 1 84898 771 5   978 1 84898 772 2   978 1 84898 773 9

Some titles from Level 5

978 1 84898 775 3   978 1 84898 776 0   978 1 84898 777 7

978 1 84898 779 1   978 1 84898 781 4   978 1 84898 782 1

An Hachette Company
First Published in the United States by TickTock, an imprint of Octopus Publishing Group.
www.octopusbooksusa.com

Copyright © Octopus Publishing Group Ltd 2013

Distributed in the US by
Hachette Book Group USA
237 Park Avenue, New York NY 10017, USA

Distributed in Canada by
Canadian Manda Group
165 Dufferin Street, Toronto, Ontario, Canada M6K 3H6

ISBN 978 1 84898 780 7

Printed and bound in China
10 9 8 7 6 5 4 3 2 1

All rights reserved. No part of this work may be reproduced or utilized in any form or by any means, electronic or mechanical, including photocopying, recording or by any information storage and retrieval system, without the prior written permission of the publisher.